For Holly and Ove,
where it all started; with love

Illustrations © 2011 by Pamela Dalton • All rights reserved • No part of this book may be
reproduced in any form without written permission from the publisher • Library of Congress
Cataloging-in-Publication Data available • 978-1-4521-0470-6 • Book design by Mai Ogiya
Typeset in Society Page • The illustrations in this book were rendered in cut paper and
watercolor • Manufactured by C&C Offset, Longgang, Shenzhen, China, in August 2011
10 9 8 7 6 5 4 3 2 1 • This product conforms to CPSIA 2008 • Chronicle Books LLC
680 Second Street, San Francisco, California 94107 • www.chroniclekids.com

# THE STORY OF CHRISTMAS

From the King James Bible
Illustrations by Pamela Dalton

HANDPRINT 🖐 BOOKS
an imprint of Chronicle Books • San Francisco

**I**n the days
of Herod, the king of Judea,
there was a virgin espoused
to a man named Joseph. She
lived in the city of Nazareth;
and her name was Mary.

And the angel Gabriel was sent from God unto her, and said, Hail, thou that art highly favored, the Lord is with thee: blessed are thou among women.

Fear not, for thou shalt bring forth a son, and shalt call his name Jesus.

He shall be great, and shall be called the Son of the Highest; and of his kingdom there shall be no end. And Mary said, Behold the handmaid of the Lord; be it unto me according to thy word.

And the angel departed from her.

And it came to pass in those days,
that there went out a decree from
Caesar Augustus that all the world should
be taxed. So all went to be taxed,
every one into his own city.

And Joseph also went into Judea,
to be taxed with Mary his espoused wife,
being great with child.

And so it was, that, while they were there,
in the city of David, which is called
Bethlehem, the days were accomplished
that she should be delivered.

And she brought forth her firstborn son, and wrapped him in swaddling clothes, and laid him in a manger; because there was no room for them in the inn.

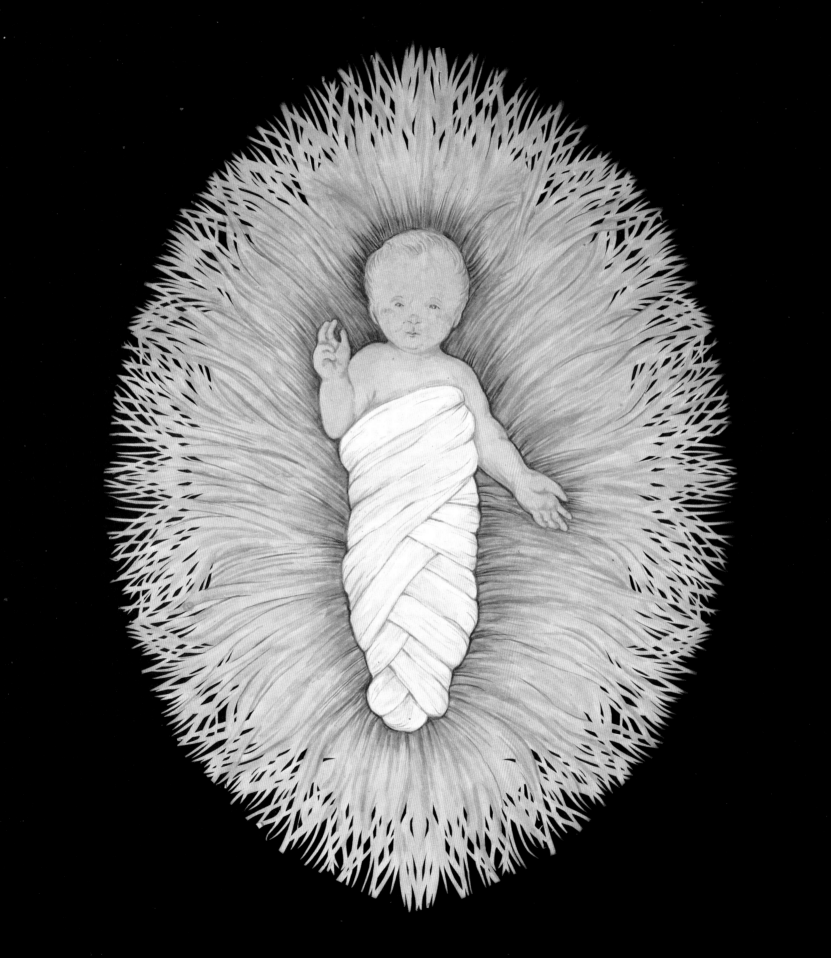

And there were in the same country
shepherds abiding in the field,
keeping watch over their flock by night.

And, lo, the angel of the Lord came upon
them, and the glory of the Lord shone round
about them: and they were sore afraid.

And the angel said unto them,

Fear not: for, behold,
  I bring you good tidings of
    great joy, which shall be
      to all people.

  For unto you is born this day
    in the city of David a Savior,
      which is Christ the Lord.

    And this shall be a sign unto you;
      Ye shall find the babe wrapped in
        swaddling clothes, lying in a manger.

And suddenly there was with the angel
a multitude of the heavenly host praising God,

and saying, Glory to God in the highest,
and on earth peace, good will toward men.

As the angels were gone away from them into heaven, the shepherds said to one another, Let us now go even unto Bethlehem, and see this thing which the Lord hath made known unto us. And they came with haste, and found Mary, and Joseph, and the babe lying in a manger.

And when they had seen it, they made known abroad the saying which was told them concerning this child. And all they that heard it wondered at those things which were told them by the shepherds.

Now when Jesus was born in Bethlehem of Judea in the days of Herod the king, behold there came wise men from the east to Jerusalem, saying, Where is he that is born King of the Jews? For we have seen his star in the east, and are come to worship him.

When Herod the king had heard these things, he was troubled, and all Jerusalem with him. Then Herod, when he had privily called the wise men, enquired of them diligently what time the star appeared.

And he sent them to Bethlehem, and said, Go and search diligently for the young child; and when ye have found him, bring me word again, that I may come and worship him also.

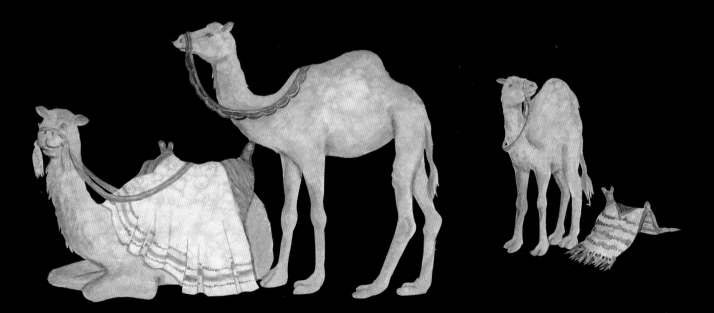

When they had heard the king, they departed; and, lo, the star which they saw in the east, went before them, till it came and stood over where the young child was.

And they saw the young child with Mary his mother, and fell down, and worshipped him and when they had opened their treasures, they presented unto him gifts: gold, and frankincense, and myrrh.

And being warned of God in a dream
that they should not return to Herod, they
departed into their own country.

And behold, the angel of the Lord appeareth to Joseph, saying, Arise, and take the young child and his mother, and flee into Egypt; for Herod will seek to destroy him. When he arose, he took the child and his mother, and departed into Egypt.

But when Herod was dead, Joseph took the young child and his mother, and returned to Nazareth.

And the child grew, and waxed strong in spirit; and the grace of God was upon him.